Booboo's Dream

Story by
Paul Cline

Pictures by
**Paul Cline &
Judythe Sieck**

A Peter Smith Book for
MEDLICOTT PRESS

Thanks to Cooper Edens for his "tail" end.

For the dreams we all have.

—P.C.

For our beloved Moby whose spirit sings eternally.

*Thanks to B. Hockenstein for helping to
draw back the curtain and thanks to
Michele for the light.*

—J.S.

Text copyright © 1990 by Paul Cline
Illustrations copyright © 1990
by Paul Cline & Judythe Sieck
1 3 5 7 9 10 8 6 4 2
First Edition
Library of Congress Catalog Card Number 90-62103
Hardbound ISBN 0-9625261-1-8

Manufactured in
Hong Kong

Booboo spent most of her time gazing out of the
window and wishing. "I wish I were someone different,
even just a little bit. Then life would be so wonderful."

One winter night the heat
went out in Booboo's home.
Everyone was warm except
Booboo, until Mother
wrapped her up.

Then the family began to laugh. "That's not a dog," they said, "it's an owl!" "It's a bear!" "It's a kangaroo!" "It's a tiger." "It certainly isn't our Booboo!"

"If I'm not Booboo, then I can
be all these other things,"
Booboo said to herself.
"How exciting."

That night, as Booboo slept, she dreamed. "Hello, my name's Booboo and I'm a dog." "Hoo, hoo," said the owls, and they flew away.

Booboo found she could fly too. "Now I'm an owl. If I were a dog I'd bark and the cows would chase me. That would be fun." But as an owl the cows didn't notice her.

BAM

Booboo wasn't used to being an owl. She flew too low and too fast. "It isn't much fun being an owl. I'm cold, my wing hurts, and it's snowing."

Soon the snow covered
Booboo. When it stopped,
she crawled out.

"Hello, my name's Booboo
and I'm an owl, I think."
The polar bears laughed.
"You're not an owl," they
said. "You're a strange-
looking polar bear."

"Well, I don't feel like a polar bear,"
Booboo said to herself.

Then she saw some penguins. "Oh,
penguins! I've never played with
penguins."

SPLASH

But not really being a polar bear,
she wasn't used to the ice.

"Now I'm even colder. Being a polar bear isn't much fun.
Perhaps I can swim to a warmer place?"

Booboo swam until she landed on a
beach. It was warm there. "Hello, my
name's Booboo and I'm a polar bear."
The kangaroos laughed.

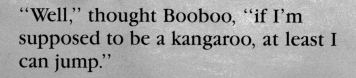

"Well," thought Booboo, "if I'm supposed to be a kangaroo, at least I can jump."

She jumped past the kangaroos,

past the koalas,

past the kookaburras.

Booboo jumped so high and so fast she jumped right out of being a kangaroo.

"Oh dear, life *was* simpler
when I was just me.

But this is fun and I do feel warmer."

Then through the trees she saw her family. "Hello, Mom. Hello, Dad. Hello, kids. I'm your Booboo; don't you recognize me? I'm not a tiger." But they ran away.

Booboo ran after them crying,
'I'm Booboo. I'm your Booboo.
Come back! Please don't leave
me!'' Booboo ran and ran.

She was still running when
she woke up. It was
morning. The heat was back
on and she had rolled out of
the jacket and scarf.

"Who am I now?" she asked herself.

When her family came down to
breakfast they called, "Hello, Booboo.
How's Booboo? Did you sleep well?

Are you nice and warm again? Oh Booboo,
we love you just as you are."

"Just as I am," Booboo said to herself.
"Yes, I *do* love being me. Just as I am."

Distributed by

GREEN TIGER PRESS

435 East Carmel Street, San Marcos, CA 92069-4362
Toll Free 1/800/424-2443
Telephone 619/744-7575
FAX 619/744-8130